SIX SLEEPY SHEEP

To our six little lambs
Jon, Todd, Jackee, Kevin, Brian, and Monica
We love ewe. — J.R.E. & S.G.T.

For Tess — J.O'B.

PUFFIN BOOKS
Published by the Penguin Group
Penguin Books USA Inc., 375 Hudson Street, New York, New York 10014, U.S.A.
Penguin Books Ltd, 27 Wrights Lane, London W8 5TZ, England
Penguin Books Australia Ltd, Ringwood, Victoria, Australia
Penguin Books Canada Ltd, 10 Alcorn Avenue, Toronto, Ontario, Canada M4V 3B2
Penguin Books (N.Z.) Ltd, 182–190 Wairau Road, Auckland 10, New Zealand

Penguin Books Ltd, Registered Offices: Harmondsworth, Middlesex, England

First published in the United States of America by Caroline House,
Boyds Mill Press, A Highlights Company, 1991
Published in Puffin Books, 1993

1 3 5 7 9 10 8 6 4 2

Text copyright © Judith Ross Enderle and Stephanie Gordon Tessler, 1991
Illustrations copyright © John O'Brien, 1991
All rights reserved

LIBRARY OF CONGRESS CATALOGING-IN-PUBLICATION DATA
Gordon, Jeffie Ross.
Six Sleepy Sheep / by Jeffie Ross Gordon;
illustrated by John O'Brien.   p. cm.
Summary: After being awakened, six sheep
try various antics to get back to sleep.
ISBN 0-14-054848-3
[1. Sheep—Fiction. 2. Sleep—Fiction. 3. Counting.]
I. O'Brien, John, 1953–   ill. II. Title.
PZ7.G6576Si 1993   [E]—dc20   92-40165

Printed in the United States of America
Set in Goudy Old Style

SIX SLEEPY SHEEP

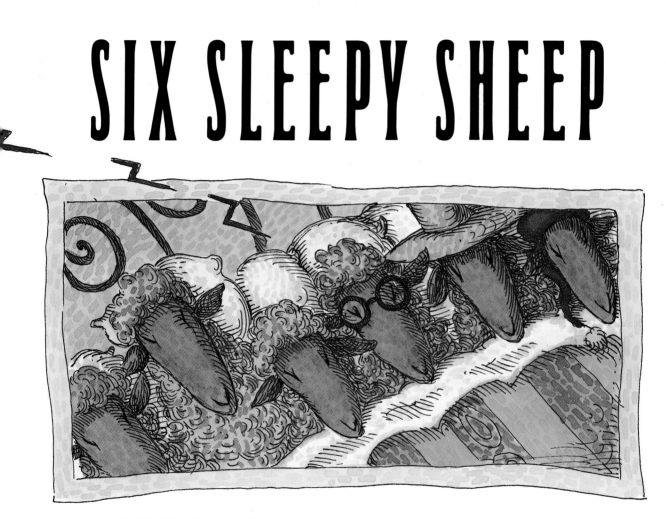

BY **JEFFIE ROSS GORDON**   ILLUSTRATED BY **JOHN O'BRIEN**

PUFFIN BOOKS

AAH! Six sleepy sheep slumbered on six soft pillows in one big bed

UNTIL...

one sheep snored.

"SHSHSH!" said five awake sheep.

And they gave that sheep a shake.

Now six sleepy sheep could not sleep.

they skipped in circles until they were swirly.

Soon one sheep snoozed.
Now five sleepy sheep could not sleep.

SO...

they slurped celery soup until they were sloshy.

Soon one sheep snoozed. Now four sleepy sheep could not sleep.

 SO...

they told spooky stories until they were shivery.

Soon one sheep snoozed. Now three sleepy sheep could not sleep.

SO...

they sang songs until they were silly.

Soon one sheep snoozed.

Now two sleepy sheep could not sleep.

SO...

they sipped simmered milk until they were snuggly.

Soon one sheep snoozed. Now only one sleepy sheep could not sleep.

SO...

he counted to seven hundred seventy-six.

Six sleepy sheep slumbered

on six soft pillows in one big bed

UNTIL...